FIRECRACKER POWER

POWER

And
OTHER STORIES

The Fairfield Friends Devotional Adventures

Firecracker Power and Other Stories
The Lightning Escape and Other Stories

9702

NANCY SPECK

A FAIRFIELD FRIENDS DEVOTIONAL ADVENTURE

FIRECRACKER POWER
And
OTHER STORIES

BETHANY HOUSE PUBLISHERS
MINNEAPOLIS, MINNESOTA 55438

Published by Bethany House Publishers
A Ministry of Bethany Fellowship, Inc.
11300 Hampshire Avenue South
Minneapolis, Minnesota 55438

Printed in the United States of America.

Library of Congress Cataloging-in-Publication Data

Speck, Nancy
    Firecracker power and other stories with take-away value /
Nancy Speck.
        p.   cm. — (A Fairfield Friends devotional adventure)
    Summary: A group of friends learn some important lessons
about practicing Christian values. Each episode is followed by
questions and suggested Bible verses.
    ISBN 1–55661–961–8 (pbk.)
    [1. Christian life—Fiction.   2. Conduct of life—Fiction.]
I. Title.   II. Series: Speck, Nancy. Fairfield friends devotional
adventure.
    PZ7.S7412Li   1997
    [Fic]—dc21   97–4710
                                                          CIP
                                                          AC

To Marta and Rachel

May you continue to grow in God.

NANCY SPECK is a free-lance writer and home-maker who has published numerous articles, stories, and poems. Her background in creative writing and social work gives her unique insight into the importance and challenge of teaching children Christian character traits at an early age. Nancy and her husband, Brian, have two elementary-age daughters and make their home in Pennsylvania.

Contents

Cameron Parker

Cameron is very smart in math and science and is in third grade at a private school, Foster Academy. He lives with his parents, older brother, Philip, and younger sister, Justine.

Ceely Coleman

Ceely, short for Cecilia, is hardworking and serious. She is in fourth grade at Morgandale Christian School, plays field hockey, and has a black cat named Snowball.

Hutch Coleman

Hutch, short for Hutchinson, is Ceely's younger brother. He's a second grader at Morgandale Christian School and is the class clown.

Min Hing

Min, a third-grade student at Fairfield Elementary, lives with her parents and grandmother. She's quiet and shy, takes ballet lessons, and plays the piano.

Valerie Stevens

Valerie lives with her mother and little sister, Bonnie, since her parents are divorced. Valerie, who is friendly and outspoken, is an average student in second grade at Fairfield Elementary.

Roberto Ruiz

Roberto, a fourth grader at Fairfield Elementary, has lived with his grandpop ever since his parents died. His older brother, Ramone, lives with them. Roberto plays soccer and has a dog named Freckles.

Firecracker Power

Hurry up, Cameron!" yelled Ceely.

"Pedal faster!" Roberto called.

Cameron pumped his legs as hard as he could. He tried to catch up to Ceely and Roberto as well as Min, Valerie, and Hutch, his friends from the Fairfield Court neighborhood. But by the time Cameron parked his bike at the pool, the other Fairfield Friends were already swimming.

I know I'm overweight, thought Cameron. But so was everyone in his family. *I wish I were more athletic so I could keep up with the others*. But he was always a block behind when they rode bikes and a lap behind when they had swimming races. *Other kids never want me on their team, either. I always make them lose.*

That evening, though, Cameron worked on

his science experiment in the basement. And he forgot all about not being good at sports. Cameron was very good at science. In fact, he was so smart that he attended a private school, Foster Academy, and took junior-high-level science and math classes.

Cameron was working on a project that involved *aerodynamics* (air-o-die-nam-iks). He tested objects of different shapes and sizes to see how fast they traveled through the air. He also used his computer to create his own drawings for aerodynamic cars of the future.

A few days later, Cameron met the other Fairfield Friends at Ceely and Hutch's house for a softball game. *Here we go again*, he thought as Roberto and Min chose up sides.

"I'll take Valerie for my team," Roberto said.

"Ceely, you're on mine," said Min.

"C'mon, Hutch," called Roberto.

Then there was silence. Min sighed. "You're on my team, Cameron."

After Min and Ceely each hit singles, it was Cameron's turn to bat.

"C'mon, Cameron!" yelled Ceely. "Hit it hard!"

Cameron spit on his hands and gripped the bat tightly. He smacked the ball on the first pitch and took off running. The ball rolled into center field and straight into Hutch's glove. He galloped toward first base and easily beat Cameron. "You're out!" Hutch yelled.

"Gee whiz, Cameron," called Ceely. "Can't you run any faster?"

"I ran as fast as I could!" Cameron yelled back.

"Not fast enough," said Hutch.

Suddenly Mrs. Coleman appeared at home plate. "Pizza's ready!"

Balls and bats and gloves dropped as the kids raced for the house.

"Hey," said Ceely, "we've got a new *Church Friends* video we can watch while we eat."

Munching on pepperoni pizza, they watched a story about a church youth group that was putting on a musical. One of the girls sang terribly. The others made fun of her. But then the youth leader flipped open his Bible. "Romans 12:6," he began. " 'We all have different gifts.' " He paused while turning pages. "And Proverbs 11:12 says, '. . . a person with understanding keeps quiet.' "

He put the Bible down and turned to the group. "Some people will have main parts," he said. "Others are needed in the chorus, and some are needed to paint the scenery. We can't all be good at the same things, but God has given each of us different talents to use. So we certainly shouldn't make fun of someone's lack of ability to do something."

The girl went on to make beautiful backdrops for the musical. All the church members marveled at them. The other kids realized she had a wonderful talent for art.

The Fairfield Friends glanced uneasily at one another while the tape rewound. Ceely, Hutch, and Min lowered their heads and stared at the floor. No one could look at Cameron. To break the silence, Roberto told them about the go-cart races he'd seen advertised in town.

"That sounds cool," said Cameron. "We could build the go-cart ourselves and enter the race as a team."

Cameron's suggestion was met with silence again. *Nothing's changed*, he thought, *even after seeing the video. They still don't want me on their team. I'll make them lose because I'm not fast enough to help push the cart.*

"Yeah . . . um . . . OK," Roberto stammered. "Let's meet at my house tomorrow and get started. I have lots of wood and crates and stuff to build it."

The next day, the Fairfield Friends, with Roberto's grandpop's help, cut boards for the base of the go-cart. Valerie brought along the wheels from her broken wagon. Min helped her put them on. Roberto placed two crates on top of the boards and nailed them on. Cameron looked at the finished cart and shook his head.

"Let's try her out!" Roberto said excitedly. "Hutch, Valerie, you two are the smallest. You guys ride inside while Ceely, Min, and I . . . and Cameron give you a push."

The friends got into position at the top of the driveway. On Roberto's count of three, they pushed the cart forward with all their strength. After the first few steps, Cameron fell behind.

When the others let go, the cart rolled slowly to the end of the driveway. Valerie and Hutch climbed out.

"Oh, brother," said Hutch. "We've got a problem. I can walk faster than this thing."

"Just great," Ceely said.

"There goes the race," said Roberto.

"All that work for nothing," added Valerie.

They stared silently at the cart. Several moments passed. Then Cameron cleared his throat. "I could make a couple of suggestions, if you want."

"Like what?" Roberto asked.

"First of all," began Cameron, "the shape of the cart is all wrong. It's not aerodynamic enough."

"Aero what?" asked Min.

"Aerodynamic," he repeated. "It has to do with how fast objects can move through the air. The cart is too boxy, so it rams into the air like into a wall. But if we round off the top and shape the front into a point, it will pierce the air like an arrow."

The other five friends looked at Cameron, speechless. "Can we do that to the cart?" Roberto finally asked.

"Sure can," answered Cameron. "Also, Valerie and Hutch should lean down in the cart so that less of their bodies hits the air, too."

The friends rebuilt the go-cart as Cameron suggested. In practice runs, it blasted down the driveway like a rocket. After some final changes, they painted the name *Firecracker* on each side.

On the day of the race, the Fairfield Friends rolled *Firecracker* to the Morgandale High School parking lot. As they lined up with the others, everyone stared at the go-cart with the rounded top and pointed front.

"Carts, take your mark. . . . GO!" yelled the starter. Valerie and Hutch ducked way down as Ceely, Min, and Roberto clutched the sides of the cart and began running. They let go, and *Firecracker* exploded down the parking lot. Cameron, waiting at the end, cheered them on.

The go-cart sailed over the finish line far ahead of the rest. The crowd roared wildly for *Firecracker*. The Fairfield Friends cheered loudly for Cameron. And Cameron smiled silently to himself.

Things to Think About

In what ways did the Fairfield Friends' words and actions hurt Cameron?

_____

_____

What did the friends learn from the video?

_____

_____

What did the Fairfield Friends later discover about Cameron?

_____

_____

Read 1 Peter 3:8; Colossians 3:12; and 1 Thessalonians 5:14–15. How should you act toward others?

_____

_____

What things aren't you good at? Read Romans 12:6a; 1 Corinthians 7:7; 12:4–6. Does everyone have the same abilities (gifts)? How can knowing this help you understand others' weaknesses as well as your own?

_____

_____

Let's Act It Out!

Memorize 1 Corinthians 7:7b.

Make a list of things you do well and keep it handy. When you are faced with something you don't do well, read through your "good" list.

_____

_____

Role-play a situation in which one person says he isn't good at something. What can another person say or do to help him and to show understanding of the other's weakness?

_____

_____

The next time you're a team captain, challenge yourself to make one of your first choices someone who is always chosen last to be on a team. Better yet, suggest choosing teams by counting off by twos.

2

9–1–1: Emergency!

"Point, two, three. Close, two, three. *Plié. Relevé.*" Min bent her knees, then rose up on her toes as Marcia, the dance instructor, called out the French ballet terms.

"That's it for today," Marcia said. "But don't forget about tryouts next week for the Spring Show."

How could I forget, thought Min as she left the dance studio. She had been practicing extra hard and hoped to get the lead part in *Waltz Bluette*. As Min changed, she imagined herself dancing in a blue *tutu*, the lacy skirt bouncing around her.

At Sunday school two days later, blue tutus still floated through Min's head as Mrs. Hall started class. "Today we're going to begin a study on prayer. Does anyone know what prayer is?"

Several hands shot up.

"Yes, Cal?"

"Prayer is when you ask God for things."

"OK. Anyone else? Linda?"

"It's also thanking God for things He has given you."

"That's correct, too," Mrs. Hall said. "In fact, the simplest meaning of prayer is talking to God. And God wants us to talk to Him every day. Turn in your Bibles to Philippians 4:6. Min, would you read the verse, please?"

Min nodded. " 'Do not worry about anything. But pray and ask God for everything you need. And when you pray, always give thanks.' "

Mrs. Hall turned to her own Bible. "And Mark 11:24 says, '. . . ask for things in prayer. And if you believe that you have received those things, they will be yours.' "

Wow, thought Min to herself, not listening to anything else Mrs. Hall said. *All I have to do is ask God for the lead part in* Waltz Bluette, *and He'll give it to me*. She began immediately. *Dear God*, prayed Min in her head, *please give me the lead in* Waltz Bluette. *Amen*.

Min prayed faithfully right up until the day

of the Spring Show tryouts. She watched Kate, Tara, and Ashley perform. They danced well, but she knew she could do better. *I've practiced really hard*, thought Min. *Besides, with all my praying, God is sure to give me the lead part.*

Then it was Min's turn. As the music began, her heart thumped and her hands sweated. Min tiptoed lightly to the center of the stage. She twirled to one corner. Then she whirled gracefully to the front. After two leaps and a toe spin, she exited the stage.

"Thank you, girls," called Marcia. "I'll post the list of parts on the board in a few minutes."

After Min left the changing room, she joined the others clustered at the bulletin board. "Congratulations, Tara," said Kate.

"Thanks," Tara said, smiling broadly.

Min couldn't believe her ears. *Tara? The lead? Get real!* But it was true. Angry tears formed in her eyes. *That's it, God,* said Min silently. *I'll never pray to you again.*

Min moped the rest of the week. That Sunday, she plodded into her Sunday school room and flopped into a back seat. Mrs. Hall noticed.

"What's the matter, Min?" Mrs. Hall asked gently as she sat down beside her.

"I prayed to God all last week for the lead in *Waltz Bluette*, but He didn't answer my prayer. He must have answered Tara Hoy's prayer instead, because she got the part."

"I'm sorry about that," said Mrs. Hall. "But as I explained last week, sometimes God's answer to a prayer is no. But that's still an answer, isn't it?"

Min shrugged. She didn't remember hearing any of that last week.

Mrs. Hall frowned, like she was trying to think of something. Then she smiled. "Suppose you asked your mom for a snack right before dinner. She'd probably say no because then you wouldn't be hungry for dinner. You didn't receive the answer you wanted, but she did answer you."

Mrs. Hall paused briefly and then continued. "And maybe you'll get the lead part next year. Isn't that still an answer to your prayer?"

"Yeah, I guess," Min mumbled. "But why doesn't God answer it now?"

"I don't know, Min, except that God answers prayers according to His reasons. And He always wants the best for each person."

Well, thought Min, *I don't care what God's reasons are, because I'm not going to pray to Him anymore anyway.*

At ballet rehearsal the next day, Min couldn't even look at Tara. After class, she waited with Kristen, an advanced ballet student who lived a few blocks from her. Kristen's mom was dropping Min off at home since her parents had gone out to dinner. Min's grandmother, who lived with the Hings, would let her in.

It was almost dark when she waved good-bye to Kristen and her mom and walked up the front steps. Min rang the doorbell twice. That was her signal so her grandmother would know who it was.

Min waited, but Grandmother didn't come to the door. She rang the bell twice again, but she still didn't come. Then she peeked in the window. There was Grandmother lying on the couch, asleep.

Why doesn't she wake up? wondered Min. All at once it hit her. *Something's wrong with Grandmother!* She banged on the window and then on the door. She pushed the doorbell over and over. "Oh, please, God," cried Min out loud. "Let Grandmother be all right! Help me get into the house!"

Suddenly a thought jumped into her brain. *The basement windows. Maybe one of them is open.* Min raced to the back of the house. She pulled at one window and then the other. They were both locked. She kicked at them, hoping they would break. But her sneakers were no match for the heavy glass panes.

"Please help me get inside, God," Min prayed again. Then, with one mighty blow, she kicked a window near the top. The latch broke, and the window flew open. "Thanks, God," she said. Min froze for a second, realizing that she had just prayed.

But then she quickly scrambled through the window, ran up the basement steps to the kitchen, and dialed 9-1-1. Soon the paramedics arrived. And Min's parents came home after she called them at the restaurant.

Grandmother was fine, the paramedics said. She had accidentally taken an extra allergy pill that made her fall into a very deep sleep.

The following week, Grandmother sat in the audience with Min's parents for the Spring Show. "Our next dance," said Marcia, "is called *Waltz Bluette*. Tara Hoy will dance the lead."

Min stared at her ballet slippers, still unable to believe she wouldn't be performing the solo. She didn't even feel like dancing her own part anymore.

"This is both a happy and sad moment for Tara," continued Marcia. "Tara's family is moving to Africa this summer, and she won't be able to take ballet there."

Min slowly looked up. She finally understood God's answer to her prayer. *So that's why God didn't answer my prayer the way I wanted. This is Tara's last chance to star in a ballet.* Tears filled her eyes as she thought of Tara's sadness at leaving ballet. *Thank you, God,* Min prayed, *for giving Tara the lead.*

When the dance was over, the audience clapped loud and long. The dancers had danced their hearts out, especially Tara . . . and Min, too.

Things to Think About

What did Min's Sunday school classmates, and later Min, learn about prayer?

_____

_____

How did Min's prayers change from the beginning to the middle and finally to the end of the story?

_____

_____

Why does God sometimes answer no to a prayer?

_____

_____

Read Mark 11:25 and 1 John 3:21–22; 5:14. What things must you do in order to have your prayers answered?

_____

_____

Read 1 Thessalonians 5:17; Ephesians 6:18; and Colossians 4:2. When and how often should you pray?

_____

_____

Read 1 Timothy 2:1; Psalm 86:12; and Luke 11:2–4. Who and what should be included in your prayers?

_____

_____

Let's Act It Out!

Memorize Colossians 4:2.

Write a prayer to say thank you to God or to tell Him how great He is.

_____

_____

_____

Start a prayer diary. Write down a request and the date. Then record when each prayer was answered and how God answered it. Don't forget to thank Him for His answers.

_____

_____

A Fairfield Friends Devotional Adventure

If you usually say a memorized prayer at mealtimes, try saying grace in your own words.

_____

_____

3

The Great Mouse Race

That's it, Hadley!" said Cameron excitedly. "Now a turn to the left. Straight ahead. OK. Now right." Cameron pushed the stopwatch button. "Yes!" he exclaimed. "Hadley, that was your best time yet. You ran the maze in just forty-three seconds."

"Hi, Cameron. What's up?" asked his older brother, Philip, as he walked into the room with his friend Keith.

"I just ran Hadley through the maze again," Cameron answered. He stroked Hadley's furry head.

"Cameron is taking a three-week science camp at the college," Philip explained to Keith. "Everyone has to teach a mouse to run a maze."

"There's a race the last day," Cameron

added. "I've been training him hard since the first day."

"Well, I hope you win," offered Keith.

"Hadley has the fastest time so far," he said.

"You want to shoot some baskets with us?" asked Philip.

"Nah. I think I'll run Hadley a couple more times," answered Cameron. He put him through the maze twice more and then locked him securely in his cage.

That evening, Cameron checked on Hadley before going to bed. Halfway through the family room, he stopped and stared. The cage door was open, and Hadley was gone.

"Oh no!" yelled Cameron. "Hey, everybody. Come here, quick!"

Footsteps pounded from different areas of the house. Philip, Cameron's younger sister, Justine, and both his parents ran into the family room.

"What is it, Cameron?" asked Mom.

"Hadley is gone," said Cameron, pointing to the cage. "But I know the latch was tight when I put him back."

"I guess I didn't latch it tightly," said Philip.

Cameron wheeled around and looked at Philip. "What do you mean?"

"Well, when Keith and I were done playing

basketball, we came in here to watch TV. Keith wanted to see Hadley. We got him out, just for a minute. But . . . I guess the door wasn't shut right." Philip paused. "I'm really sorry, Cameron. I know how important he is to you."

"Well, you should have been more careful," Cameron answered angrily.

"Hold on, guys," said Dad. "Did it occur to anybody that he is probably in the house somewhere?"

They quickly split up and began a careful search of the house. A half hour later, Cameron called everyone to the laundry room. He showed them the hole chewed through the dryer hose, which led to the outside.

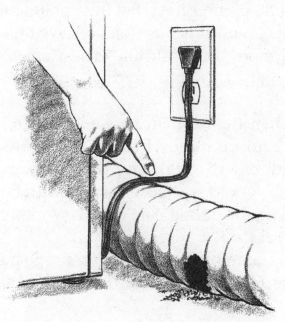

"Hadley's gone for good," said Cameron.

"These things happen," said Dad. "It was an accident."

Cameron glared angrily at Philip and stomped from the room. *Accident or not*, he thought, *I'll never forgive Philip.*

The next day, Cameron brought home Muffin from the college. He put her in the beginning of the maze with a piece of cheese at the end. At every corner she turned the wrong way. She ran back to the start twice. When Muffin finally reached the cheese, Cameron checked the stopwatch. It had taken her two minutes and twenty-five seconds.

Cameron knew he could never teach her the maze in three days. But he kept her running it right up until it was time to leave on Friday. "One more time, Muffin," said Cameron. He looked at his watch. He could just make it to class.

When he finished, he stuck Muffin in her cage and charged through the house. He thundered through the living room, past Justine, who was almost finished with her 500-piece jigsaw puzzle. She'd been working on it for weeks.

As Cameron passed, Muffin's cage bumped the card table. It leaned up on two legs, and the entire puzzle slid to the floor.

"Cameron!" shrieked Justine. "Look what you did!" She was almost in tears.

"Well, you shouldn't have put the card table right there," Cameron shot back.

"There's plenty of room. You could have been more careful."

"It's just a puzzle, Justine. Get a grip. Now I'm really late." He slammed the front door behind him and ran toward the college.

As Cameron feared, Muffin came in dead last in the maze races. But even worse, the winning mouse won with a time that was ten seconds slower than Hadley's best time.

I know he would have won, thought Cameron as he trudged through the hall after class. Suddenly he stumbled. He looked down to see an untied shoelace. Cameron put down the cage and bent to tie his shoe. He grabbed each string and yanked hard. A shoelace broke. He slid to the floor and began tying the pieces together. As he worked, Cameron began to focus on someone talking in the room a few feet in front of him.

"We, of course, know God forgives us our sins. But you must help the people in your church understand the main point: Since God has forgiven us our mistakes, we must forgive others when they do something wrong to us."

What's this about? wondered Cameron. *It sounds like some class is being taught to ministers.*

"As it says in Colossians 3:13," the voice continued, " 'Do not be angry with each other, but forgive each other. If someone does wrong to you, then forgive him. Forgive each other because the Lord forgave you.' "

Cameron paused for a minute, then finished tying his shoe. "Well, maybe I'll forgive Philip someday," he muttered under his breath. "But not yet." His shoestring fixed and tied, Cameron picked up Muffin and continued home.

When he opened the front door of the house and walked into the living room, he saw Justine at the card table. She had started her puzzle all over again. She looked up at Cameron, a mixture of anger, hurt, and sadness in her eyes.

And suddenly Cameron understood. *That puzzle was really important to her, just like . . .* Cameron sighed and walked over to his sister.

"I'm sorry, Justine," he said softly, "for wrecking your puzzle."

Justine wiped her eyes. "It's okay," she answered. "I know it was an accident."

As Cameron walked away, he also realized

that apologizing to Justine wasn't enough. He had more to do. As he searched the house for Philip, Cameron asked God to forgive him for not having a forgiving heart.

He found Philip on the back porch. Philip looked up from the book he was reading but didn't say a word.

"Look, Philip," began Cameron in a rush. "I know you didn't purposely leave Hadley out of his cage. It was an accident and . . . so . . . I forgive you."

There was a pause. "Thanks," said Philip. "And again, I'm sorry." He paused once more. "How did Muffin do today?"

"She came in last," Cameron answered.

"Yeah, maybe," said Philip, putting his book down. "But if I help you train her the rest of the summer—"

"She'll be unbeatable by the Fall Science Fair," Cameron interrupted excitedly.

"C'mon then," said Philip. "Let's get started."

"It'll have to wait until after dinner," said Cameron. "Right now I'm going to help Justine with her puzzle."

Things to Think About

Why was Cameron mad at Philip?

_____

_____

What made Cameron realize that he should forgive Philip?

_____

_____

Why did Cameron need to ask God for forgiveness just as he needed to ask Justine?

_____

_____

Read Romans 12:17–19. Should you ever "repay" or "punish" people when they wrong you?

_____

_____

Whose responsibility is this?

_____

_____

Read Matthew 6:14–15; Luke 6:37; and Ephesians 4:32. Why should you forgive others?

_____

_____

Read 1 John 1:9 and Romans 6:22–23. Why do you need God's forgiveness?

_____

_____

Let's Act It Out!

Memorize Colossians 3:13.

Read the following examples. What should you do about forgiveness in each?

1. You're mad at your sister because she ate the last popsicle.

_____

_____

2. You knocked over your mom's flowerpot and broke off part of the flower.

_____

_____

3. You told a lie to your teacher about forgetting your homework.

_____

_____

4. A friend broke your toy while playing with it.

_____

_____

5. You made fun of someone and made her cry.

_____

_____

6. You got angry with God because He didn't answer a prayer the way you wanted.

_____

_____

7. You picked a fight with your brother because you're angry about a bad grade.

_____

_____

8. Your mom accidentally threw out a magazine you wanted to keep.

_____

_____

9. You spilled a drink on your dad's report for work.

_____

_____

10. A classmate bumped into you in the cafeteria, making you drop your tray.

_____

_____

11. You decided not to work on your memory verse for Sunday school this week.

_____

_____

12. Your baby sister crawled into your room for the third time today and messed it up.

_____

_____

With a parent's permission and help, bake a family "forgiveness cake" (recipe on next page). Plan a family sharing time so that everyone has the chance to talk about any problems with forgiveness. Or share the cake as a special devotion time where your family remembers the things that God has forgiven them for.

Forgiveness Cake

Preheat oven to 350°. Grease and flour a 9×13 pan. Place all ingredients in a large mixing bowl. Mix on low speed for one minute, scraping bowl constantly. Beat on high speed for three minutes, scraping sides of bowl occasionally. Pour into prepared pan. Bake in oven for 30–35 minutes, or until toothpick inserted in center comes out clean. Cool and frost with your favorite icing.

F 2 cups **F**lour
O 3 teaspoons baking p**O**wder
R 1 cup **R**egular milk (whole, 2%, 1%, or skim)
G 1 ½ cups **G**ranulated sugar
I 1 **I**nteresting ingredient* (see below)
V 1½ teaspoons **V**anilla
E 1 **E**gg
N ½ cup **N**uts, optional
E 1 **E**gg
S 1 teaspoon **S**alt
S ½ cup **S**olid shortening

*Interesting ingredients—add to cake mix, if desired: ½ cup finely chopped maraschino cherries; 2 teaspoons maple flavor; 2 teaspoons powdered instant coffee; 2 tablespoons grated orange peel; ½ cup shaved semi-sweet chocolate; or 1 cup flaked, toasted coconut.

4

Lost in the Mountains

The Fairfield Friends bounced up and down as the school bus wound through the mountains. The kids from all the churches in Morgandale were on their way to Laurel Lake Camp.

"Are you excited for camp?" Ceely asked Valerie.

"You bet," said Valerie. "I can't wait for the swimming races and horseback riding."

After arriving at camp, Valerie, Min, and Ceely each settled into their assigned cabins. Then they met at the lake, along with the other campers, for swimming instructions and races.

When it was Valerie's turn, she swam freestyle, switched to the breast stroke, and then rolled over and did the back crawl.

"Wow," said Sharon, the instructor. "You're a great swimmer!"

"I know," said Valerie. "I have the fastest times in my age group on the swim team back home."

Soon it was time for the races. The campers listened as Sharon explained they should swim to the first water marker, turn, and swim back. But Valerie wasn't paying attention. She was busy stretching her muscles and daydreaming about winning the race.

"This'll be a cinch," she said to Min and Ceely when she joined them at the edge of the lake.

"Swimmers, take your marks. . . . GO!" shouted Sharon. Eight girls swam away. Within a few strokes, Valerie was in the lead. But when she reached the first marker, she swam on to the second. By the time she swam back to shore, she was in last place.

Valerie climbed out of the water and stomped over to Sharon. "I thought you said the second marker was where we should turn. You didn't make the rules clear. It wasn't a fair race."

"No one else misunderstood the turning point," said Ceely.

"We both heard you say the first marker," Min said to Sharon.

Valerie grabbed her towel and stormed

away without another word.

After supper, the campers gathered at the fire ring in front of a log stage. The counselors put on a skit about some students at a cooking school who were training to be chefs. One student, Marvin, who already had some practice, bragged to the others about what he knew about cooking.

For the final test, each student had to prepare a dish following a recipe he'd never seen before. When the teacher tasted Marvin's dish, he almost choked. Marvin had misread the recipe. Instead of half a teaspoon of hot mustard, he'd put in two whole ones. Marvin failed the course.

"The lesson to be learned here," explained Mr. Potter, the camp director, "can be summed up in two Bible verses. James 4:16 says, 'But now you are proud and you brag. All of this bragging is wrong.' And Proverbs 16:18 says, 'Pride will destroy a person. A proud attitude leads to ruin.' "

Ceely and Min looked at Valerie.

"What are you looking at me for?" Valerie questioned, frowning at them.

"That skit sounded a little like you today," said Ceely.

"I wasn't bragging," snapped Valerie. "I was

stating a fact. I am a good swimmer."

"Yeah," Min said softly. "But you lost the race."

The next day, Valerie's cabin was scheduled for horseback riding after dinner. They met at the stables where Mike, the stable hand, saddled the horses and helped the girls mount.

When he got to Valerie, he took her arm to help her on. "Oh, I know all about horses," she said, mounting her horse easily. "I have a horse at my dad's farm."

"I can see you've been around horses," Mike said. "Maybe you'll ride in a competition someday."

"I'd like to," said Valerie. "My dad's teaching me to jump, too. I'm getting really good at it."

Soon Mike and the eight girls were plodding onto the trail that led through the mountains. Valerie was last in line. *How can I show the others how good I am at riding horses if I'm behind them?* she wondered. Then Valerie had an idea.

As the riders rounded a curve ahead, Valerie reigned her horse to a stop until the others were out of sight. Then she took a trail to the right. *I'll beat them back to the stables. They'll really think I'm a good rider then.*

After a ways, the trail forked into two more. Valerie chose one, but farther on it stopped altogether. Valerie headed back toward the main trail, but she was all confused. Before long, she was lost.

As Valerie searched for signs of the trail, she heard a rustling in the leaves near her. She looked down and saw a black snake slither out from behind a rock. Valerie's horse, frightened by the snake, reared up on his hind legs. Valerie desperately tried to hold on. But her horse bucked and jumped so hard that she lost her grip and flew right off of him.

''Owww!'' Valerie cried as she hit the ground on her side, her wrist bending under her. She sat up slowly and felt her wrist. It hurt horribly and was beginning to swell. *Now I can't ride anywhere. I'll have to wait for someone to come find me.* She stood up and angrily kicked her foot in the dirt. *I've never been thrown off a horse before.*

Valerie hoped help would come soon. Darkness was already creeping into the thick woods on the mountains, and she was getting scared. She tried not to cry as she sadly thought of the others meeting around the bright fire for more skits.

All at once, last night's skit returned to her mind. So did the Bible verses. Valerie began to cry, sad with herself now.

Suddenly she saw a bobbing light. Then she heard a whinny, and a horse galloped up. Mike hopped off and ran to her. "Valerie, are you OK?"

"I think so," she said. "But I sprained my wrist. I can't ride."

Mike helped Valerie onto his saddle. Then he guided both horses onto the main trail and back to camp.

Valerie told the director and the nurse what happened. "I'm sorry I didn't stay on the trail."

"Well, it's a good thing you didn't hurt more than your wrist," said the nurse. "But I'm afraid you'll have to keep your arm in a sling. Swimming and riding are off your activity list."

Valerie nodded silently.

On the last night of camp, everyone gathered at the fire ring one last time. Mr. Potter said it was time to recognize the wonderful counselors who had spent their summer working at the camp.

"Sharon, our swimming instructor, was a great teacher. What you don't know is that she is a champion swimmer. She took the summer off from competition to recover from an injury. But this winter she'll be training for the National College Championships."

All the campers clapped. Valerie stared at the fire.

"And next is our horseman, Mike," continued Mr. Potter. "He owns his own stables in Littleton and is a former champion jumper. We're pleased to have him as our stable hand."

The campers clapped again. Valerie continued to stare at the burning logs.

The next day, while the campers loaded onto the bus, Valerie looked silently out the window. She saw Sharon and Mike sitting on a picnic table and talking.

Valerie got off the bus and walked up to them. "Thanks for all your help this week," she said, smiling for the first time in days. "I learned a lot about swimming and riding . . . and a whole lot more."

Things to Think About

Why did Valerie lose the swimming race and hurt her wrist?

_____

_____

Because of her hurt wrist, what couldn't Valerie do the rest of the week?

_____

_____

Read Matthew 23:12 and Proverbs 18:12. What did Valerie learn about herself?

_____

_____

What does the Bible say will happen if you brag or are proud?

_____

_____

Read Philippians 2:3–4. What did Valerie learn about Sharon and Mike? According to these verses, how did they handle their ability to do things well?

_____

_____

Read Luke 18:9–14. How can you be great and bring honor to yourself?

_____

_____

Let's Act It Out!

Memorize Matthew 23:12.

Think of something you aren't so good at. Pretend someone who is good at it brags to you about her success in this area. Act out this conversation with someone. Write down or tell how you felt.

_____

_____

_____

_____

Draw a picture of something you're good at. At the bottom, list some ways you can put Philippians 2:3–4 into practice.

5

The Final Count

"Good morning, students," said Mr. Drum. "And welcome back to school."

Ceely and Hutch sat with their classes in the church sanctuary for the first chapel service of the year.

"We have a special visitor with us today," Mr. Drum continued. "Mr. Shank of International Missions is with us from South America, where he and his wife are missionaries."

Mr. Shank told them they had started a small church in a poor village. But the people were so busy just trying to find enough food to eat each day that many didn't care about church. Even the house Mr. Shank and his wife lived in had no running water. He told them they got their water from a well in the village.

It was often dirty and sometimes made them sick.

"But my wife and I try to be like the servants in 2 Corinthians 6:4 by 'accepting many hard things, in troubles, in difficulties, and in great problems.' Because as 1 Corinthians 15:58 says, we know that our 'work in the Lord is never wasted.' "

Mr. Drum returned to the podium. He explained that for this year's service project, they would all learn to be workers for God. Money they earned doing chores and jobs for family, friends, and neighbors would be put toward a goal of $800. This would be enough for International Missions to purchase eighty new Bibles to be used wherever they would be needed most.

"I encourage you to get your friends involved, too," he said. "More workers means getting more done for God."

Ceely and Hutch looked at each other across the sanctuary. They knew they were both thinking the same thing. The rest of the Fairfield Friends could help with the project!

That Saturday, Roberto, Valerie, Min, and Cameron met at the Coleman house. They had each received a call from Ceely or Hutch during the week.

"So how did everybody do?" asked Hutch.

"I weeded the garden for my grandmother," said Min. "Here's $2."

"I cleaned out the garage for my dad," answered Cameron. "It took me two evenings to do it, so my dad gave me $5."

Roberto spoke up next. "Valerie and I helped the janitor empty the trash from all the school classrooms. He gave us a dollar each."

"That's $9 altogether," said Ceely. "And added to the $5 Hutch and I made, that makes ... $14."

"And your school wants to earn how much?" asked Roberto.

"The goal is $800," said Hutch.

The friends looked at one another silently and then stood up. "OK," said Ceely. "Let's go to Plan B. Servant teams, meet back here in two hours."

Ceely, Hutch, and Roberto went one way. Cameron, Valerie, and Min headed off the other.

"Let's try that house," suggested Hutch, pointing to the one they were passing. "Their car looks really dirty. It's got bug guts all over it."

They rang the bell and explained their work for the service project to the lady who answered the door. They offered to wash her car for whatever she wanted to pay. She said she wasn't interested.

They walked on to another house with overgrown flower beds. The owner agreed to let them pull weeds. Excited, they got to work. Hutch scraped his arm on a rosebush. He danced and jumped around the yard, holding his arm in the air. Roberto laughed at him, but Ceely was too busy sneezing because of her allergies to some of the flowers.

When they finished an hour later, they were tired, sweaty, and dirty. But they proudly

showed the man their work. He paid them each a quarter.

When they arrived at the Coleman house, they learned that Valerie, Cameron, and Min hadn't done much better.

"We only earned $3," said Cameron. "And for mowing this huge lawn!"

"And I got stung by a bee," Min said quietly.

"Altogether we made only $3.75," said Valerie. "What a waste of time."

They were quiet for a moment. Then Ceely spoke. "Maybe we didn't make much," she said, "but the missionary said that work for God is never wasted."

"And we should be servants for God even when things don't go right," added Hutch.

"So let's try again next week," suggested Min. "Maybe we'll have better success."

And did they ever. They washed cars, walked dogs, emptied trash, and painted a fence. The Fairfield Friends made $15.

The following Friday, Ceely and Hutch took $32.75 with them to school. They divided the money between them to give to their teachers. But it was never collected. Ceely and Hutch learned why after arriving in the sanctuary for a special chapel service.

"I know you've been eagerly waiting to see

whether we've reached our goal of $800," said Mr. Drum to the students. "This year, instead of each class submitting its total, we're going to turn over your money one at a time. But this isn't a contest. What I want to show you is that even the smallest amount, when added to the rest, is worth much. OK, now. Kindergarten."

One at a time, the ten students in kindergarten handed their money to Mr. Drum. He counted it and put it in a large basket. Then he called out the amount to Mrs. Taylor, the school secretary. She wrote the number down on a blackboard that had been brought into the sanctuary. As each grade went forward, the total kept growing. It climbed from $325 to $550 to $715.

The fourteen eighth graders rose. This was the last class, their last chance. The sanctuary was completely still and quiet except for Mr. Drum's voice. "Here's $14.50. $20. And $8.25."

The students watched Mrs. Taylor add each amount on the blackboard.

"Another $18. $6.75. $15." The total now stood at $798.50.

Heather Harmon, smiling broadly, handed Mr. Drum her money. "It's $12."

The students burst into a roar. And when the rest of the eighth graders had turned in their money, the grand total stood at $846.35. That was more than enough for International Missions to purchase eighty new Bibles.

Ceely and Hutch called the rest of the Fairfield Friends after school to tell them the good news. But their friends had some exciting news of their own. They had been asked back by some of the neighbors to do more work for them. And they could keep this money that they earned. The Fairfield Friends, though, agreed they would each place some of what they earned in the church offering each week.

But the biggest surprise came a few weeks later. Ceely and Hutch called everyone to meet at their house after school. When everyone arrived, Ceely pulled out a paper.

"This is a copy of a letter from the director at International Missions. He sent the letter to the school, and Mr. Drum made a copy for everyone to take home. 'Dear Morgandale Christian School,' " Ceely began. " 'We greatly appreciate the money you earned from your service project. Half of the eighty Bibles we purchased with it were sent to a missionary in England. The others were sent to a large city where a new pastor is starting a church in a poor neighborhood. Another Christian school sent money to buy wood and tools to fix up an old building for him to hold services in. Three other churches joined together and sent enough money to start a soup kitchen in the front of the building. Once a week, people in the neighborhood can come and receive food for their bodies. And with the use of your Bibles, they receive the most important food there is: God's Word for their souls. Thank you and God bless.' "

Ceely folded up the letter and shoved it back into her pocket. Then the Fairfield Friends talked excitedly, making plans for more work they could do for God.

Things to Think About

How were the Fairfield Friends servants or workers for God?

_____

_____

What problems did they have?

_____

_____

What was the Christian school service project able to do when everyone helped out even a little?

_____

_____

What added reward did the Fairfield Friends receive that would also help others?

_____

_____

Read Colossians 3:23–24 and Ephesians 6:7. Who should you do your work for? How should all of your work be done?

_____

_____

Read 2 Corinthians 6:1, 4, 6 and 1 Peter 4:10.

How else can you show you are a servant of God?

_____

_____

Let's Act It Out!

Memorize 1 Corinthians 15:58.

Arrange to do some chores for your parents or neighbors and put some of the money in your church offering. Or save a larger amount and give it to missionaries or a charity.

_____

_____

Have your Sunday school, church, or youth group do a service project, maybe working together with other churches. Make sure you share the Gospel as part of your project.

Remembering the Bible verses above, list some ways you can be a good servant for God.

_____

_____

6

Rotten Eggs

What are you going to be for the costume party tomorrow?" Valerie asked Min and Roberto as they walked home from school.

"A princess," Min answered. "What about you, Roberto?"

"I'm putting padding around my arms and legs and going as a body builder," he said. Roberto made a muscle.

"Ooh, look at that muscle," said a voice.

"Showing off to the girls, are we?" said another voice.

Roberto, Min, and Valerie looked behind them. Four boys on bikes rolled up beside them. They were Roberto's soccer buddies.

"Cut it out, guys," said Roberto. "We were just talking about costumes for our school party."

"Well, you can talk about that later," said Josh. "Right now we have some really important stuff to discuss."

"Are you with us?" Tony asked.

"Or do you want to stay here with your girlfriends?" asked Brad, laughing.

Roberto thought a second and then climbed on the seat behind Josh. As they rode down the street, Josh told him they were planning to throw eggs at houses the next night. They had gotten the idea from Brad's older brother, who had egged some houses with his friends the week before.

"But that might ruin the paint on the houses," said Roberto. "It really isn't right to hurt someone else's property."

The other boys looked at one another and sighed.

"Oh, don't get religious on us now," said Josh. "The people can clean off the egg before it does any damage."

The four stared at Roberto, waiting for his reply.

"Yeah, well . . . I guess so," Roberto mumbled.

The next evening, just as it was getting dark, Roberto met the others. They parked their bikes at the end of a street, and Brad handed each boy an egg from some cartons in his bike basket. Then they slinked through the shadows of trees and bushes until they reached the first house.

Crack! went an egg on the garage door. *Smack! Splat!* Several more smashed on the side of the house. Roberto looked at the egg in his hand. He threw it toward the house, but he didn't even aim.

The boys moved on to other houses and continued to throw eggs. Roberto's eggs kept missing. Josh noticed.

"Are you blind?" he asked Roberto as they sneaked up to a house. "How can you miss a house? Or maybe you're just chicken?"

"I am not," said Roberto. He threw an egg angrily at the garage door. It hit with a bang and splattered.

"That's more like it," Brad said.

They rode to another street. At the first house they came to, Roberto stopped.

"Hey, not this house, guys," he whispered. "Mrs. Thompson lives here. She's an old lady who goes to my church."

"So what?" Tony said. "She can get a neighbor to clean up."

They threw eggs at Mrs. Thompson's house and some others until they were out of eggs. As

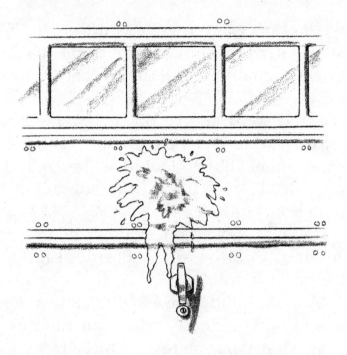

they headed home, everyone laughed . . . except Roberto.

The next day Roberto trudged into his house after school. He hadn't slept well the night before and had been tired all day.

"What's this world coming to?" Grandpop said, shaking his head as he hung up the phone.

"What's wrong?" Roberto asked.

"That was Mrs. Cook. She just heard that Mrs. Thompson fell off a ladder while trying to wash egg off her garage door. Some kids probably threw them last night as a prank. She's stiff and sore now and can't get the egg off."

Roberto nodded silently and went to his room. He was still there when his grandpop called him to supper. He explained he wasn't feeling well, didn't want supper, and was going to bed early.

Roberto put his pajamas on and fell onto his bed in the dark. His dog, Freckles, hopped up beside him and licked his face. Then he curled up, closed his eyes, and went to sleep. Roberto closed his eyes, too. But he couldn't sleep at all.

A short time later, he heard the voice of his brother, Ramone, in the kitchen. Roberto leaned up on an elbow. Freckles changed his position. *What's Ramone doing home?* Roberto wondered. *He always eats with friends at the college on Friday night and hangs out with them until late. But it's only*—he looked at his clock— *7:30.*

Roberto got up and opened his bedroom door a little. Ramone and Grandpop were talking in the kitchen. He sat on the edge of the bed and listened.

"I just didn't know what to do," said Ramone. "My friends wanted me to go along. But I didn't think it was right."

"It sounds to me like you *did* know what to

do," said Grandpop. "You obeyed God rather than men."

Ramone chuckled. "Acts 5:29," he said. "That's one of the verses that stuck in my head when I decided not to go with them. The other was James 4:17."

Ramone and Grandpop began the verse together. " 'And when a person knows the right thing to do, but does not do it . . . ' "

" 'Then he is sinning,' " Roberto said softly, finishing the verse from his bed. Grandpop had made him memorize this verse and others, just as he had Ramone.

"Dear God," prayed Roberto, "forgive me for what I did, and help me to obey you. Amen." He rolled over next to Freckles and fell asleep.

In the morning, Roberto got up early and went out to the kitchen. Grandpop was making coffee.

"Feeling better?" he asked.

"Yeah, I think so," Roberto answered. "But I don't know for how long." He took a deep breath. "Grandpop, I was one of the kids who threw eggs at Mrs. Thompson's house. I'm really sorry. I knew it was wrong, but I did it anyway. The other guys made fun of me and

. . . and . . . I just gave in." Roberto choked back tears.

Grandpop frowned at him. "Your soccer friends?" he questioned.

Roberto nodded.

"I've told you before they aren't the type of friends you should have," continued Grandpop. He paused. "But why are you just now telling me about this?" he asked sternly.

"Last night in bed I was reminded of some Bible verses," Roberto answered. "I've asked God to forgive me."

"I'm glad," said Grandpop. "That makes it right with God. And God has forgiven you. But that doesn't make it right with Mrs. Thompson, does it?"

Roberto shook his head.

After breakfast, Roberto hopped on his bike and pedaled to Mrs. Thompson's house. When she answered the door, he quickly confessed to his part in the egg throwing.

"I'm really sorry you hurt yourself. I've come to clean off any remaining egg and to paint your garage door. And I can give you the names of the other boys who did—"

"Hush, Roberto," said Mrs. Thompson. "God saw who did it. And He will hold them responsible for their actions."

Roberto nodded in understanding.

"So then, you can find a bucket and some paint in the garage," said Mrs. Thompson.

Roberto was soon busy cleaning the egg off the garage. Suddenly he heard voices.

"Boy, are you stupid," said Josh as he rode up to the end of the driveway. "What'd you tell for? We got away with it."

"Yeah," agreed Tony. "No one can prove we did it. No one saw anything."

"And if you rat on us," Matt said, "we'll just say we didn't do it."

Roberto whistled as he worked, ignoring the boys. Finally they rode on down the street. Roberto picked up his brush and began to paint, knowing he was doing the right thing.

Things to Think About

Did Roberto really want to throw eggs at the houses? How do you know?

_____

_____

Why did he go along with the other boys anyway?

_____

_____

What did Roberto overhear that helped him admit to his grandfather and then Mrs. Thompson that he had been part of the egg throwing?

_____

_____

Read John 14:23; 1 John 5:3; and Psalm 119:9–11. If you love God, what should you do?

_____

_____

Read Proverbs 15:3. Who knows when you obey or disobey?

Read 1 John 3:7 and Psalm 119:133–134.
What should you be careful of?

Read Psalm 119:129–130 and Deuteronomy
11:18–19. Why is reading and memorizing
Scripture important?

Let's Act It Out!

Memorize Acts 5:29.

Make a list of actions you can take to help
you make a right decision when faced with
pressure to do something wrong.

Start a Scripture memory notebook. Select
Bible verses from this book, from Sunday
school lessons, or others that you want to

learn. Write out the verse and reference on a page of the notebook, one for each week of the year. Go over the verse each day and say it by heart to your parents at the end of the week.

7

Guilty as Charged

M in and Roberto marched up the steps to the state museum with the rest of the third and fourth graders from their school.

"Look!" said Min, pointing in front of her. "There's Cameron."

After catching up to him inside, they learned that his class was touring the museum, too. The two boys talked excitedly about what they would see.

"Shh," said Min. "The guide is starting to talk."

"We have a lot of rooms to see in the museum today," said a young man in a blue museum uniform. "We'll be touring this part of the building first. Since there are several other groups here, please stay with me. And don't enter any rooms that have a rope across the doorway. They aren't open for visitors at this time."

He turned and led the group down a hall. The first room was filled with displays about the state's history. Min, Roberto, and Cameron looked at old maps. The guide showed them old tools that the early settlers in the state had used.

As they left the room, Min suddenly needed to use the rest room. In her excitement over the field trip, she had forgotten to stop there before leaving school.

Min found her teacher, Mrs. Stake, and whispered to her. She pointed the way to the bathroom. As the group continued down one hall, Min turned down another and entered the rest room.

A few minutes later, as Min walked quickly up the hallway to rejoin the group, she heard a loud crash. Suddenly, two boys and a girl bolted from a room. They were from Min's class. The three of them skidded to a stop when they saw her. Then they turned and ran up the hallway.

As Min passed by the room, she noticed a rope hanging from one side of the doorway. Inside the room she saw a broken vase. Pieces of it lay all over the floor.

After Min found her group, she slipped between Cameron and Roberto. She whispered to them what had happened.

"Well, you didn't actually see them break the vase," Roberto whispered back. "You better not say anything."

"Yeah," agreed Cameron. "No one has to know anything."

"Shh," a teacher said to the three of them.

As Min boarded her bus to go back to school, the three classmates told the others what had happened at the museum. They made sure everyone knew Min had seen them.

"We all have to agree not to say anything," said Susie.

"If no one rats on us, we can get away with it," said Paul.

"Yeah," agreed Ryan.

All three of them stared hard at Min as they spoke. Min heard their warning loud and clear.

The next day, the school principal waited in Min's classroom as the students entered. He told them that the museum director had called to report that a valuable vase had been broken. A museum guard had found it while making his rounds. The museum guides said that their class had been in that part of the museum when it happened.

"If anyone heard or saw anything, he or she needs to report it. Meanwhile," he continued, "the school must pay for the damage. The money will come out of the field trip fund, so all future field trips are cancelled for now."

After school, Min didn't wait for Roberto and Valerie. She'd had a stomachache ever since the principal's announcement that morning and wanted to hurry home. As she picked up the mail at the front door, she brightened a bit. Her new *Church Friends* magazine had come today.

After a quick hello to her grandmother, Min settled herself in a chair with her magazine. First she worked the Bible crossword puzzle. Then she read a story about a boy and his dog. The dog had dug up a bunch of flowers in the neighbor's yard. The boy had seen his dog leave the yard, his feet covered with dirt and flower petals. But since no one else had seen him, he decided not to say anything. That way his dog wouldn't be blamed.

At the end of the story, Proverbs 12:17 was written out. "An honest witness tells the truth," read Min, "but a dishonest witness tells lies." Min closed the magazine. She knew what she had to do.

On the way to school the next day with Valerie and Roberto, Min filled in Valerie on what had happened. She also told them about the magazine story.

"I guess Cameron and I were wrong," said Roberto. "I never thought that not saying anything about something that's happened is the same as if you actually tell a lie about it."

"Me neither," said Valerie. "Either way you're being dishonest."

Min nodded and then sighed. They had arrived at school. She opened the door to the school and walked slowly down the long hall to the principal's office.

"Class, I have an important announcement to make," said Mrs. Stake after the bell rang. "Take your seats, please." When everyone was seated, she began.

"A witness came forward this morning to tell what happened at the museum. It looks as if three students from our class will be working off the cost of the damage for the vase to repay the school. Field trips will be rescheduled, but these students will not be able to attend any the rest of the year."

Min could feel the burning stares of her classmates and friends. At recess, everyone ignored her. At lunch, no one sat with her. After another recess spent alone, Min slumped in her seat. She didn't even perk up when a special guest arrived.

"Class, this is Detective Williams," said Mrs. Stake. "I've asked him to come talk about his job as part of the community helpers we've been learning about in Social Studies."

Detective Williams talked about his police training and about the types of crimes he had to solve. When he finished, he asked the class if there were any questions.

"What was the hardest case you ever solved?" asked Paul.

Detective Williams thought a minute. "I'd have to say that it was a series of robberies that happened a few years ago. A man was blamed for them, but there really wasn't any proof that he did it. Finally, just before his trial, a woman came to me. She said she had seen her neighbor carrying several of the stolen things into his house from his car. But he was a local businessman and respected in the city. She was afraid that people would be angry with her if she accused him."

Detective Williams paused. "Turned out he had committed all the robberies. Thankfully this woman was honest and spoke up, or an innocent man might have been sent to prison."

At afternoon recess, several girls asked Min to join in their jump rope game. After school, Haley asked Min if she could come over to play the next day. As they talked, the girl who had broken the vase walked by, purposely bumping into Min. "Excuse me, rat," she said in an angry voice.

Min and Haley looked at each other and laughed.

"I'll see you tomorrow, then," Haley said.

"Yeah, OK," answered Min.

Haley ran to her bus. Min hurried across the playground to catch up with Valerie and Roberto, eager to tell them about her afternoon.

Things to Think About

Why did Min keep quiet about what she saw?

_____

_____

Why did Min finally tell the truth?

_____

_____

What helped most of her classmates realize that she had done the right thing by telling what she saw?

_____

_____

Read Proverbs 6:16–19. What "thing" does God dislike so much that He mentions it twice?

_____

_____

Read Acts 5:1–4. If you are dishonest, who are you really being dishonest to?

_____

_____

Read Proverbs 12:22; 2 Corinthians 8:21; and Ephesians 4:25. When you tell the truth, who does it make you right with?

_____

_____

Let's Act It Out!

Memorize Proverbs 12:17.

Play "The Honesty Game." Number slips of paper from 1–12. As each person draws a number, he or she must tell how someone should act in that situation.

1. Your brother and a friend are horsing around and break a lamp. He tells you to go along with his story that he accidentally tripped and knocked it over. If you don't, he'll tell your parents about the scissors cut in your bed spread that's covered with a stuffed animal. What should you do?

2. While in the bathroom at a friend's house, you break the soap dish. What do you do?

3. You're watching a favorite TV show, and

your mom asks if your homework is done. It's not, but you know you can finish it in the morning on the bus. What should you tell her?

4. A store is giving out balloons to children six years old and under. You turned seven a week ago and you're small for your age. You really want a balloon. Should you get in line for one?

5. You're taking a timed test in school. You are to put your pencil down when the buzzer rings. When it does, you see that you have only two more questions and the teacher isn't looking your way. What should you do?

6. You accidentally trampled your mom's new flowers. She blames the cat. What do you do?

7. A lady at the grocery store is giving out free cookie samples. A sign says "One cookie per person." You take one and eat it. A few minutes later, she leaves and a new lady takes over. Since she wouldn't recognize you, you could get in line again

for another cookie. What should you do?

8. It's field day at school, and since you have a sprained ankle, you've been asked to help with the scoring. Some classmates ask you to help them win by making their race times faster and adding a few inches to their distances in the broad jump. What do you tell them?

9. You're supposed to read a certain book for a book report. The book is also out on video. Watching the video would take only two hours while reading the book would take much longer. What do you decide to do?

10. An unpopular girl has been blamed for writing on the bathroom wall. You know that your best friend did it because she told you she did. She also told you not to tell anyone. Should you tell?

11. The worst batter on the team is up next. The coach tells the umpire that the boy isn't feeling well even though he's fine. Since you're one of the best hitters, he

puts you in to bat in his place. What would you do?

12. You bring home a pack of school papers to show your parents, but two of them have low grades. You know you can take out these two papers and bury them in the garbage can on the way into the house. What should you do?

8

Stage Fright

B ible study is over, Roberto. It's time for refreshments," said Grandpop.

Roberto looked up from the book he was reading. "OK, Grandpop."

A few minutes later, Roberto passed out brownies and pretzels to the Bible study members seated in the living room. Mr. Ruiz followed with a tray of coffee and tea.

"I have some wonderful news," said Mr. Hogan, putting down his coffee. "You remember Mr. Jackson, who we've been praying for and who I've been sharing the Gospel with?"

"He's a co-worker of yours, isn't he?" asked Grandpop.

Mr. Hogan nodded. "Right. I've been telling him how God sent His Son, Jesus, to save us from our sins so we can have eternal life.

Yesterday he agreed to come to church with me on Sunday."

"How wonderful," said Mrs. Berry. The others then shared some times they had told people about Jesus over the years.

Roberto sat at the kitchen table nibbling on a brownie. He listened closely. He had tried to tell his soccer friends about God, but they'd always laughed at him. *Maybe I'll try again*, he thought, encouraged by the stories he had just heard.

On the way to school the next day, Roberto told Valerie and Min about what he'd heard at the Bible study.

"I always get so scared to talk about Jesus," said Min. "I never know what to say."

"Just tell them the truth," said Valerie. "I think I'll give it a try today."

"Same here," said Roberto. "I'm going to say something to the guys at soccer practice."

The next day, they shared what happened. Min told them that she had read her new Christian mystery at lunch. A classmate asked her about it. "I just didn't know what to say. I didn't even tell her the book was about learning to trust God." She sighed.

Valerie said that she hadn't done much better. She and three classmates had been making a map of Columbus's voyage. "Tom said that Columbus must have been scared as they sailed. I told him he probably trusted God. Then I told them all how they better believe in God or He wouldn't take them to heaven. They glared at me, then turned their chairs together and ignored me."

Roberto shared how he spoke to Brad at soccer practice after learning Brad had hurt his ankle. "I told him I'd pray for his ankle to heal and that he could ask God for help, too. But, as usual, he laughed at me and told me to give up the 'Jesus junk.' "

The three looked at one another. "Boy, we sure bombed," said Roberto glumly.

After school, Roberto found his brother, Ramone, at the kitchen table. He was sorting a stack of Gospel tracts. That evening, he and some others were going to hand them out to students at the college.

"Hi, Roberto," he said. "How's school going?"

"Awful," answered Roberto. He told Ramone about his, Valerie's, and Min's failed attempts to tell the kids at school about God.

"Well, I'm glad you tried," Ramone said. "But you all made a few mistakes in the way you did it." He dug in his backpack sitting on the floor and pulled out his Bible. "First Peter has some good verses on witnessing." He thumbed through the pages. "Here we go. First Peter 3:15. ' "But respect Christ as the Holy Lord in your hearts." Always be ready to answer everyone who asks you to explain about the hope you have. But answer in a gentle way and with respect.' "

He looked at Roberto. "Min should have been better prepared to share the Gospel. And Valerie was too harsh in the way she told it."

"But I spoke up and did it gently," protested Roberto.

"Yeah, but you've been telling those guys about God forever. Maybe it's time to stop talking for a while and show them instead." He turned back a page in his Bible. "First Peter 2:12 says, 'So live good lives. Then they will see the good things you do, and they will give glory to God on the day when Christ comes again.'"

Roberto shared the verses with Min and Valerie the next morning. At lunch, Min said grace before she ate. The same friend who'd asked about the book asked her why she prayed. Min, who had planned some things to say, said a quick prayer and then shared with her about God.

Valerie apologized to the three classmates at recess about being so pushy. She explained that she just wanted them to understand how important it is to know about God. This time the classmates listened. Valerie didn't know if what she said did any good. But at least she'd tried . . . gently.

At soccer practice, when a make-up game was scheduled for Sunday, Roberto spoke up. He told the team and the coach that he wouldn't be able to play because he would be in church.

The following week, preparations for the school's Thanksgiving assembly began. As always, each class did a skit about the first Thanksgiving or presented something they were thankful for. And for this particular assembly, individuals or groups of students could present their own songs, poems, or plays about Thanksgiving. The school performed the program twice, once for the students and then in the evening for parents, friends, and neighbors.

"Why don't we do something for the assembly that would tell everybody about God?" Roberto suggested as they walked home.

"We don't have very much time to plan," said Min. "Do you even have any ideas?"

"Besides, what good will it do?" asked Valerie.

"I've got it all figured out," Roberto said. They spent the next two hours at Roberto's house working on their project.

On the Tuesday evening before Thanksgiving, Valerie, Roberto, and Min waited offstage with the other students. The audience clapped loudly after each group. Finally, it was their turn. They walked to the podium, each holding a sheet of paper.

"This is a Thanksgiving poem," said Roberto. "It's titled 'Things We're Thankful For.'" The three of them took turns reading, saying the last line together.

"I am thankful for the chance to learn
I am thankful for the sun, trees, and waves
I am thankful for a home, food, and
     clothes
I am thankful for Jesus who saves
I am thankful for parents to raise me
I am thankful for music to sing
I am thankful for God's lovingkindness
We are so thankful for everything."

They left the stage to the sounds of soft, polite clapping. The three of them exchanged glum glances.

When everyone was finished performing, Roberto, Min, and Valerie met their families in the cafeteria for juice and cookies. Min's parents and grandmother, Valerie's mom, and Roberto's grandpop and Ramone stood in a group together.

A woman came up to them as they talked. "Excuse me," she said.

"Oh, hello, Mrs. Karns," said Roberto's grandpop. He introduced his neighbor to the others. "I'm glad you decided to come."

"Thank you for inviting me," she said. "I really enjoyed the program." She paused and fidgeted nervously. "Mr. Ruiz . . . um . . . well, you've also invited me to your Bible studies before, but I always turned you down. Tonight, though, I've been reminded about the blessings I've received from God all these years." She turned and smiled at Roberto, Min, and Valerie. "Would it be okay if I join you at your next Bible study?"

"It certainly would be," Mr. Ruiz answered.

Roberto, Min, and Valerie grinned at one another—and then at Ramone, who winked back.

Things to Think About

What mistakes or problems did Roberto, Valerie, and Min have when they first tried to tell others about God?

_____

_____

How did each of them solve these problems?

_____

_____

What happened because of their Thanksgiving poem?

_____

_____

Read Acts 1:8; 22:15; and Romans 15:20. What kind of people should you tell about God and Jesus? Where should you tell them?

_____

_____

Read 1 Corinthians 2:1, 4; Ephesians 6:19–20; and Colossians 4:3–4. Do you need fancy speech and big words to tell people the Gospel? How can you get over your fears of talking to others about Christ?

_____

_____

Read Matthew 5:14–16 and 1 Peter 2:12. How else can you share your faith besides talking to people?

_____

_____

Read Acts 2:46–47. What can happen when you tell people about Jesus?

_____

_____

Let's Act It Out!

Memorize 1 Peter 3:15.

Look up John 3:16 and Romans 5:8. Now write down your own version of the Gospel as well as other things about God. (For example: God created the world. God answers prayer. God doesn't like sin.) Memorize them. Be prepared to say these things when given the chance.

_____

_____

Firecracker Power

Bow your head, close your eyes, and say grace before you eat your lunch at school or when your family eats at a restaurant.

Read a Christian children's book at school or on the bus. Be ready to tell what it's about, making sure to include the "God parts." Or use it for a book report for school.

9

Secret Presents

Ceely and Hutch ran across the school playground where Valerie waited for them to walk home. Soon Cameron arrived from his school as well.

"Where are Min and Roberto?" Ceely asked as they started down the block together.

"Min's at ballet, and Roberto had a dentist appointment," answered Valerie.

"Are they still planning to meet at the shelter next Saturday?" Hutch asked.

"Yeah, I think so," Cameron said.

Each year at Christmas, the families in Fairfield Court collected canned goods. On the Saturday before Christmas, they distributed them at Safe Harbor, the homeless shelter in Morgandale.

"How awful to get food as your Christmas

present," said Ceely, shaking her head. "I'm sure glad we're not poor."

"Same here," agreed Cameron.

The four friends continued to chat about the games, dolls, and science equipment they hoped to get for Christmas. Soon Cameron turned down his street, and then Valerie hers. As Hutch and Ceely neared their house, they saw their dad's car in the driveway.

"What's Dad doing home?" asked Hutch.

"Beats me," Ceely answered, shrugging.

They walked up the drive and into the house. Ceely scooped up Snowball, her black cat, as she and Hutch entered the living room. But she quickly put the cat down when she saw their parents sitting on the sofa. Mom's eyes were red and teary. They had never seen Dad look so sad.

"What's wrong?" asked Ceely. "Dad, why are you home in the middle of the day?"

"Ceely, Hutch, sit down, please," said Dad. "We need to talk to you."

Ceely and Hutch each sat in a chair, never taking their eyes off their father.

"I'm home because I was laid off at work today. My boss said business might pick up again by summer, but for now, I don't have a job."

Ceely and Hutch were quiet for a few seconds as their father's words sank in. Then the questions poured out.

"But what about school?" asked Ceely. "And the new sneakers I need and the sweater with a hole that you said we would replace?"

"And what about the paper and markers you said you would get so I can make Christmas cards?" Hutch asked.

"And what if you don't go back to work?" continued Ceely, her voice rising. "How will we live?"

Dad looked at Ceely, who had tears in her eyes, and then at Hutch, who was biting his lip and staring at the floor. He picked up his Bible from the coffee table and flipped through some pages.

"Luke 12:22," said Dad. " 'Jesus said to his followers, "So I tell you, don't worry about the food you need to live. Don't worry about the clothes you need for your body." ' "

Dad turned some more pages. "Hebrews 13:5 says, 'Keep your lives free from the love of money. And be satisfied with what you have. God has said, "I will never leave you. I will never forget you." ' " Dad laid his Bible down and turned to his family. "God knows what we need to live," he said. "And He will provide for us. But it's up to us to be content with whatever we are given."

Dad continued. "Since my unemployment money won't cover the cost of Christian school, your mother is going to take a part-time secretary job to pay for it. But we'll have to carefully watch our other costs. Hutch, you'll have to be happy with your crayons for now."

"Ceely," said Mom, "we'll look for sneakers at the secondhand shop. And we can sew up the hole in your sweater."

Ceely stared at her feet. She'd have to wear used sneakers.

"Will we get anything new for Christmas?" Hutch asked.

Dad smiled. "I'm sure there will be a few things . . . but not as much as usual."

"Let's remember, though," added Mom. "Christmas is about giving to others, just as God gave the gift of His Son to us. That's enough of a present for us all."

The next day, Mrs. Coleman drove Ceely and Hutch to a store called "Wear It Again." There were two pairs of sneakers in Ceely's size. Both were scuffed, and neither were the popular kind everyone wore at school.

Ceely frowned as she stomped to the cash register with her mom to buy one of the pairs.

"Why couldn't I have had a growth spurt last month?" she mumbled.

When they got home, Hutch worked half-heartedly on some Christmas cards. He showed them to Ceely.

"They're OK," she said flatly. But they both knew how markers would have made them brighter and better.

The following Saturday, the Colemans met the other Fairfield families in the lobby of Safe Harbor. The cans of food were divided and placed in boxes. Ceely and Hutch picked up a box with a six on it and headed down the hall to apartment six.

They shivered slightly and wrinkled their noses. The shelter was drafty and smelled musty. A baby cried from somewhere. They stopped outside door number six and knocked.

A woman dressed in a faded blue sweat suit opened the door and stared at them.

Hutch and Ceely tried to smile. "Merry Christmas," they said together.

"We're from the Fairfield Court neighborhood," offered Ceely.

The woman smiled slightly. "Please come in," she said. "You can put the box on the table."

They walked into the tiny room. A girl and

boy about Hutch's size sat on the floor. The boy was drawing on the back of a paper bag with a pencil. The girl sneezed and wiped her nose. The room was terribly cold, yet she wore only a thin shirt.

"Thank you for the food," said the woman.

"You're welcome," said Ceely and Hutch. They walked silently back to the lobby.

Three days later it was Christmas. The Coleman family gathered around the small tree they had bought and put up on a table. A few brightly decorated presents sat under the tree. Hutch opened one with his name and found two large pads of drawing paper.

"Thanks," he said. But he was speechless when he opened another package and saw a box of colored pencils and a box of twenty-four brilliant markers. He pulled one out and began to draw on a piece of paper.

Ceely opened her presents and found a new sweater and a pair of pants. "Oh, Mom," she exclaimed, "they're beautiful! And my old sweater will match these pants, too. Thank you."

That afternoon, after a delicious Christmas dinner, Ceely and Hutch disappeared into Ceely's room with wrapping paper and bows. Snowball followed, chasing a strand of ribbon. A while later they approached their parents in the family room.

"Mom, Dad," said Ceely. "Could you drive us to Safe Harbor?"

"Whatever for?" asked Dad.

"We have some Christmas gifts to deliver," Hutch answered.

Mom and Dad looked at each other and smiled.

After arriving at Safe Harbor, Ceely and Hutch walked quietly to room six. They placed the presents—the new sweater, the markers, and one pad of paper—on the floor in front of the door. Then they knocked loudly and ran quickly down the hall.

Back at home, Dad started a fire. Ceely put her new pants away and got out her old sweater. Mom showed her how to mend the hole. Then Hutch got out his remaining pad of paper and the colored pencils he kept. As they sang carols around the fire, Ceely sewed while Hutch drew a picture of them all. The Coleman family had never been more content.

Things to Think About

Who did Ceely and Hutch give gifts to?

_____

_____

What gifts did they give, and why did they give them these gifts?

_____

_____

_____

How did Ceely and Hutch's attitude and feelings about what they had change during the story?

_____

_____

Read Luke 12:22–31. Why shouldn't you worry about what you have or don't have?

_____

_____

Read 1 Timothy 6:9–11. What "riches" should you be after?

_____

_____

Read 1 John 3:17–18 and 1 Timothy 6:17–18. If you have a lot of money or things, how should you use what you have?

_____

_____

Read Philippians 4:11–13. What is the secret of being content?

_____

_____

Let's Act It Out!

Memorize Hebrews 13:5.

Give your outgrown clothes and toys that are still in good shape to a shelter or other social service agency that can use them.

Collect canned goods and other items that don't spoil (pasta, rice) and secretly leave them with a family that needs it. Suggest that others in your church, school, or town do the same.

At Christmas or your birthday, make a list of what you want. Then cross out half of it.

10

Trapped on the Ledge

Valerie yawned as she walked into the living room. "Morning, Mom," she said. "How's Bonnie?"

"Her cold is pretty bad," Mom answered.

"I guess that means we can't go to Sunday school and church," said Valerie.

"I'm afraid not," said Mom. "It's so cold and damp outside. I shouldn't take Bonnie out even to drop you off at the church." Mom paused. "But you could walk over to Ceely and Hutch's church and attend services with them."

An hour later, Valerie sat on a long church pew between Ceely and Hutch. After the choir sang and the offering was taken, Pastor Sherman turned to the large Bible in the pulpit. "Joshua 1:9. 'Remember that I commanded you to be strong and brave. So don't be afraid. The Lord your God will be with you everywhere you go.'

"This week we will continue our study of Bible characters who have shown great strength in God by learning about Joshua," he said. "He asked God for strength to help him lead the Israelites into the land He promised them."

Valerie listened closely to the sermon. She wrote down the Bible verse, too.

After church, when Valerie and the Coleman family walked outside, they were greeted by swirling white flakes. Mr. Coleman insisted on driving Valerie home. As they rode through the heavy snow, Valerie, Ceely, and Hutch worked at memorizing Joshua 1:9.

That afternoon, while Valerie helped her Mom make peanut butter cookies, it snowed even harder. "I wonder if it's snowing this hard at Dad's farm?" Valerie said as she flattened balls of dough with a fork.

"Probably more," Mom answered, "since it's up in the mountains a bit."

"I'll bet I can go sledding next weekend," Valerie said happily. Then she looked at her mom. "But what about Bonnie? If she's too sick, I won't be able to have my weekend visit."

Mom smiled. "You visit your father. He'll understand if Bonnie can't come this time."

Valerie grinned. "Thanks, Mom." Suddenly Valerie had an idea. "Do you think I could have some friends go along since Dad wouldn't have to watch Bonnie all the time?"

"There's one way to find out," answered Mom, handing the phone to her.

That weekend Valerie, Ceely, Hutch, Roberto, Cameron, and Min piled into the Colemans' van. Mr. Coleman had offered to drive all the Fairfield Friends to Mr. Stevens' farm in the country. After arriving at the farm, the six friends wasted no time in getting ready to sled.

"Stick to the path across the pasture, Valerie," said her dad. "It will take you to the hills by the pond. You'll recognize the area. I took you riding there last summer."

Valerie nodded. "I remember."

"There are also some good hills on the other side of the woods, down by the old orchard. Be careful and keep an eye on the weather. It looks like another storm could blow in."

"We will," said Valerie.

The friends grabbed the sleds they had brought along and a toboggan from the barn. Then they started across the meadow. After arriving at the first group of hills, they took turns on the sleds and toboggan, packing the snow down hard. With each run they flew faster down the hill. Later on, as they walked to the hills by the orchard, it began to snow.

"We better head back soon," said Valerie.

"We came all this way, though," said Ceely. "Let's at least do that one big hill over there," she suggested as she pointed.

"All right," agreed Valerie. "But make it quick. Why don't you use the toboggan?"

"But we can't all fit on it," said Roberto.

"I don't need to go," said Valerie.

"Me neither," Cameron said. "I'm too pooped to climb another hill."

Min, Roberto, Ceely, and Hutch hiked the hill and settled themselves on the toboggan. "Here we go," they yelled together.

The toboggan started off slowly, but it picked up speed as it slid. Soon they were flying out of control down the hill, right toward the rocky edge.

Valerie saw the rocks first. "Watch out!" she screamed.

Ceely leaped to the side, landing hard in the snow. But the toboggan, with Min, Roberto, and Hutch still on it, disappeared over the side.

Valerie scrambled up the hill to Ceely. "I

think I sprained my ankle," Ceely said, holding back the tears. "But I'm OK otherwise."

Valerie nodded and climbed to the rocky ledge where the toboggan had flown off. She crawled carefully to the edge and looked over. She saw her friends on a ledge ten feet below.

"Are you all right?" Valerie yelled.

"I am," called Hutch. "But Min scraped her head. It's bleeding. And Roberto hurt his arm. He thinks it's broken."

"I'm going for help," yelled Valerie.

She slid back down the hill to Ceely and

Cameron. "Can you walk at all?" Valerie asked Ceely.

"I don't think so. You go on without me."

"C'mon, Cameron," said Valerie.

"Why don't I stay here with Ceely?" suggested Cameron. "So she's not alone."

"Go all that way by myself?!" asked Valerie.

"I'll just slow you down anyway," Cameron said. "Besides, you know the way. You can do it. You have to."

Valerie looked at them. Without a word, she turned and began striding through the snow. She tried to run, but the deep snow tired her. She slowed to a walk, but it was snowing so hard now she could barely see. The snow cut into her cheeks like icy claws.

Where are the woods? wondered Valerie. *I should be there by now.*

She marched on. Up ahead Valerie finally saw the outlines of trees. She wound through the woods, shielding her eyes from the snow. When she came into the clearing, she didn't recognize a thing. *Oh no! I must have made a wrong turn somewhere.*

Valerie turned back into the woods, trying to find a familiar landmark. She walked and walked. Finally, too tired to move, she collapsed under a tree and began to cry. *I can't do this*, she thought. *I'm completely lost and I'm so tired. I can't go on. But everyone is depending on me. I wonder if this is how Joshua felt,* she wondered.

"Joshua!" cried Valerie out loud. "How could I have forgotten?" She paused and repeated Joshua 1:9 to herself. "OK, God," Valerie said. "I can't do this myself. I need your strength and help to be brave and to find the way back."

Valerie took a deep breath and pushed herself to her feet. She looked around carefully. All at once, she saw a dead pine tree. She knew she had passed it on the way to the hills. She gathered all her strength, hurried to it, and found their footprints. Then she retraced them through the snow. Before long, Valerie arrived at the pond. After climbing over a small hill, she saw the lights of the farmhouse.

Four hours later, after a trip to the hospital, Valerie and the rest of the Fairfield Friends sat around the fireplace. They each held a mug of hot chocolate. Min had a large bandage on her head, Roberto's arm was in a cast, and Ceely's ankle was wrapped.

"It's a good thing your dad and that rescue team on snowmobiles got to us when they did," said Roberto. "I sure was getting cold."

"Yes, but thanks to Hutch we weren't scared," said Min. Hutch stood up and bowed.

"How come?" asked Cameron.

"Hutch told us about Joshua and a Bible verse he heard in church last week about having strength in God," Min explained.

"Hey, Ceely," Cameron said. "That sounds sort of familiar." He turned to the others and explained. "Ceely told me the same thing, and that helped us to be strong until help came."

"Well, anyway, we have Valerie to thank for being brave and bringing back help," said Ceely.

They lifted their mugs. "Here's to Valerie," they all said.

"No," said Valerie, smiling and lifting her mug to join them. "Here's to Joshua . . . and the Fairfield Friends."

Things to Think About

Why did Valerie get scared and discouraged?

_____

_____

Why did she become strong again?

_____

_____

Why were the other Fairfield Friends strong
and brave?

_____

_____

Read Psalm 28:7; 31:24; and Isaiah 40:29–31;
41:10. What does God give you if you ask
Him for help in time of need?

_____

_____

Read Jonah 2:1–7; Hebrews 11:1, 32–34; Proverbs 3:5–6; and 2 Timothy 3:15–16. In what
ways can you get strength from God?

_____

_____

Read Joshua 1:1–9. How did God's words
strengthen Joshua?

_____

_____

Let's Act It Out!

Memorize Joshua 1:9.

Play this "Luck of the Draw" game that focuses on finding strength in God. Number slips of paper from 1–12. Take turns drawing a number and reading that situation out loud to the others. Then talk about why some situations are worth fewer points than others. How should you use strength in God in the 0–point examples?

1. There's a thunderstorm in the middle of the night. You scream, wake everyone up, and then hide under the covers. 0 points

2. You have to read a poem in front of your whole school. As you walk to the stage, you ask God to help you calm down and get through it. 1 point

3. You're on a camp-out, and you hear some spooky noises. You repeat a memorized

Bible verse about not being afraid because God is with you. Then you ask God to help you be brave. 2 points

4. You're taking a test and you don't know a lot of the answers. You get upset and worried that you'll fail it, so you copy the answers from your neighbor. 0 points

5. You're moving to a new town. You read the Bible for verses on trusting God and have faith that He will help you adjust and make new friends. You pray each day for courage to be friendly. 3 points

6. You've been asked to sing a small solo in the children's church choir. You're worried that you won't do well, so you tell your parents you feel sick and can't go. 0 points

7. You and a friend are playing at the playground. Your friend falls, badly scraping her knee. She's crying and says she can't walk home. You tell her that God will help her make it. 1 point

8. You sign up to run a mile in a charity

race. Halfway through the course you get really tired, so you quit. 0 points

9. Your mom has to go to the hospital for a few days. You tell her not to worry. You have faith that God will watch over her and will help you do the extra chores while she's gone. 2 points

10. You've been sick with the flu. You've asked God for strength to trust Him to heal you and to get caught up on your schoolwork. 1 point

11. Your school bus was in a minor accident with a car on the way to school. You're afraid to ride the bus now, so you beg your parents to drive you to school. 0 points

12. You've struck out twice already. You walk up to bat, trusting God for courage to try to hit the ball. When you strike out again, you walk away knowing God will be with you when you try again. 2 points

Series for Young Readers*
From Bethany House Publishers

★ ★ ★

THE ADVENTURES OF CALLIE ANN
by Shannon Mason Leppard
Readers will giggle their way through the true-to-life escapades of Callie Ann Davies and her many North Carolina friends.

★ ★ ★

BACKPACK MYSTERIES
by Mary Carpenter Reid
This excitement-filled mystery series follows the mishaps and adventures of Steff and Paulie Larson as they strive to help often-eccentric relatives crack their toughest cases.

★ ★ ★

THE CUL-DE-SAC KIDS
by Beverly Lewis
Each story in this lighthearted series features the hilarious antics and predicaments of nine endearing boys and girls who live on Blossom Hill Lane.

★ ★ ★

RUBY SLIPPERS SCHOOL
by Stacy Towle Morgan
Join the fun as home-schoolers Hope and Annie Brown visit fascinating countries and meet inspiring Christians from around the world!

★ ★ ★

THREE COUSINS DETECTIVE CLUB®
by Elspeth Campbell Murphy
Famous detective cousins Timothy, Titus, and Sarah-Jane learn compelling Scripture-based truths while finding—and solving—intriguing mysteries.

* (ages 7–10)

9611